MIAMI DOLPHINS

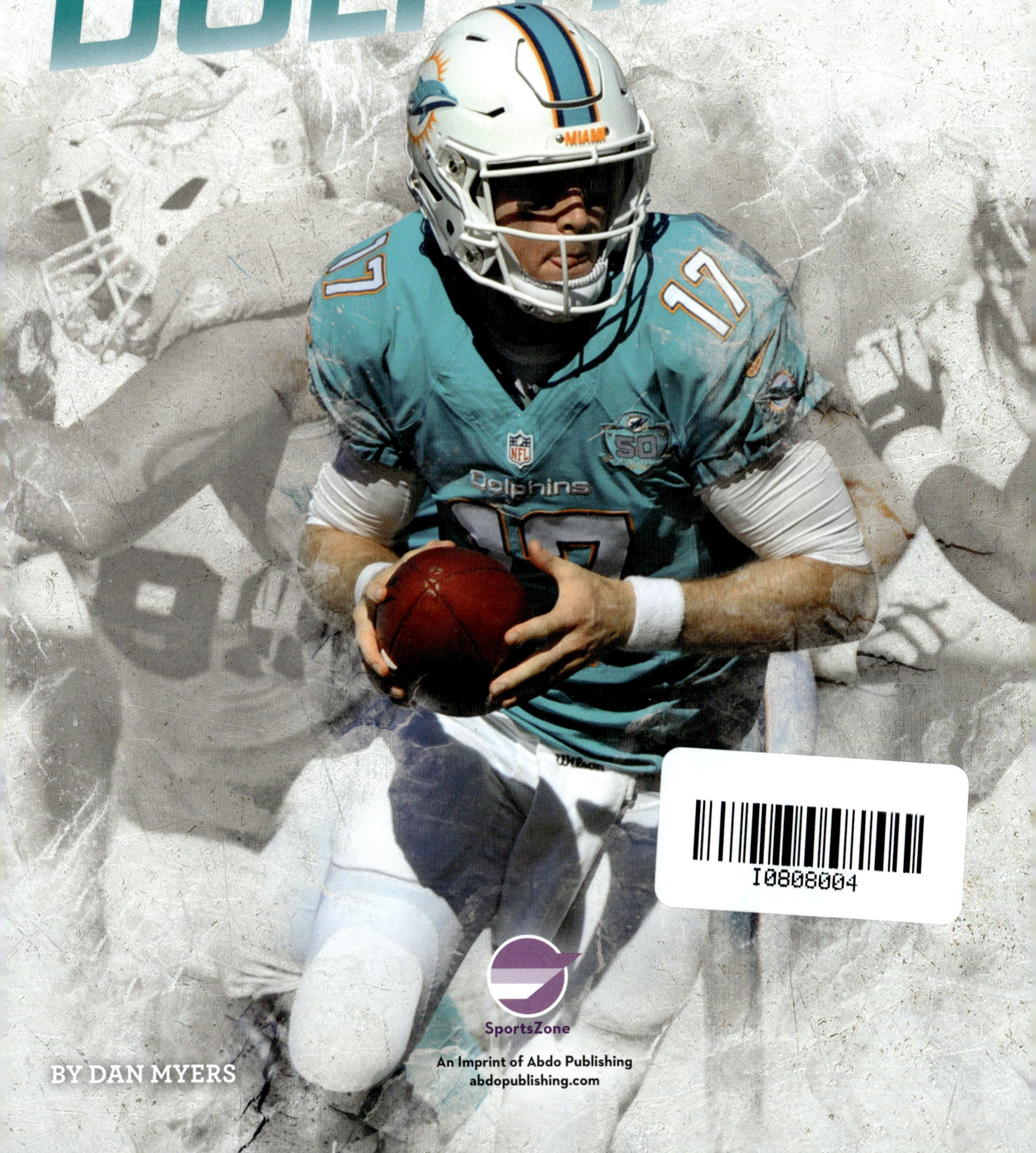

BY DAN MYERS

SportsZone
An Imprint of Abdo Publishing
abdopublishing.com

abdopublishing.com

Published by Abdo Publishing, a division of ABDO, PO Box 398166, Minneapolis, Minnesota 55439.

Printed in the United States of America, North Mankato, Minnesota
042016
092016

THIS BOOK CONTAINS RECYCLED MATERIALS

Cover Photo: Al Messerschmidt/AP Images
Interior Photos: Al Messerschmidt/AP Images, 1, 14-15, 17, 22-23, 25; Jacquelyn Martin/AP Images, 4-5; Bettmann/Corbis, 6-7; AP Images, 8-9, 12-13, 16, 20-21; Herbert Gehr/The LIFE Images Collection/Getty Images, 10-11; NFL Photos/AP Images, 18-19; Paul Spinelli/AP Images, 26-27; Bob Leverone/AP Images, 28-29; Tom DiPace/AP Images, 24

Editor: Patrick Donnelly
Series Designer: Nikki Farinella

Cataloging-in-Publication Data
Names: Myers, Dan, author.
Title: Miami Dolphins / by Dan Myers.
Description: Minneapolis, MN : Abdo Publishing, [2017] | Series: NFL up close | Includes index.
Identifiers: LCCN 2015960446 | ISBN 9781680782226 (lib. bdg.) | ISBN 9781680776331 (ebook)
Subjects: LCSH: Miami Dolphins (Football team)--History--Juvenile literature. | National Football League--Juvenile literature. | Football--Juvenile literature. | Professional sports--Juvenile literature. | Football teams--Florida--Juvenile literature.
Classification: DDC 796.332--dc23
LC record available at http://lccn.loc.gov/2015960446

TABLE OF CONTENTS

PERFECTION 4

EARLY YEARS 10

HIRING GREATNESS 14

BACK-TO-BACK 18

GETTING A LITTLE LUCKY 22

Timeline 30

Glossary 31

Index / About the Author 32

PERFECTION

It is one of the oldest legends in pro football. Every season, when the last undefeated team in the National Football League (NFL) loses, the surviving members of the 1972 Miami Dolphins celebrate.

After all, the 1972 Dolphins went undefeated. They won all 14 games in the regular season. Then they won two playoff games to reach the Super Bowl. And they won that game, too. No team had ever done that. And no team has done it since.

Members of the 1972 Dolphins still take great pride in being the only undefeated Super Bowl champion.

UNDEFEATED
72

FAST FACT

Dolphins running backs Larry Csonka (1,117 yards) and Mercury Morris (1,000 yards) became the first teammates to rush for at least 1,000 yards in the same season.

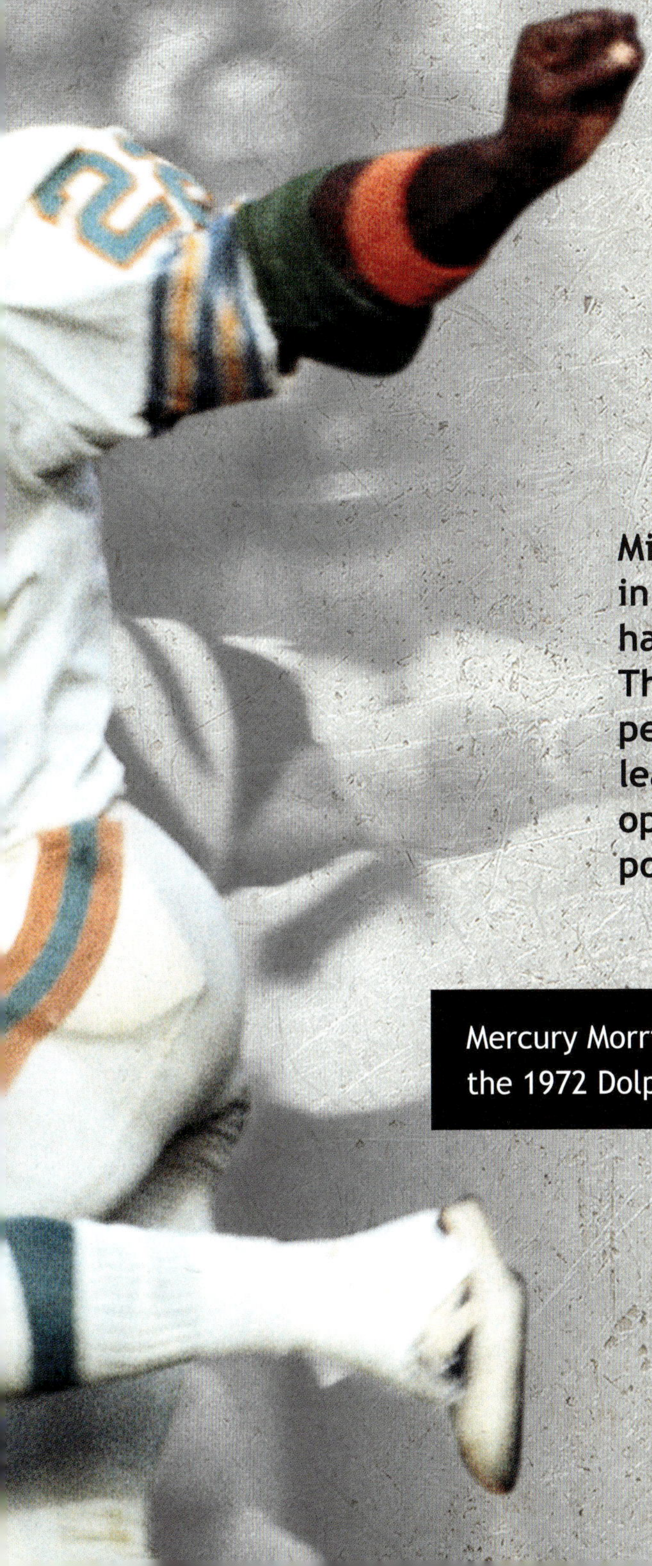

Miami's 1972 season was perfect in other ways, too. The Dolphins had the NFL's best offense. They scored almost 28 points per game. They also had the league's best defense. Miami's opponents scored fewer than 13 points per game that year.

Mercury Morris was one of the biggest stars on the 1972 Dolphins.

FAST FACT

Earl Morrall led the Baltimore Colts to the Super Bowl in 1968, but they lost to the New York Jets. He did win three Super Bowl rings as a backup with the Colts and Dolphins.

But the undefeated season came with some struggles. Starting quarterback Bob Griese broke his leg in the Dolphins' fifth game. Veteran backup Earl Morrall carried the load for the rest of the regular season.

Griese came back in the playoffs. Nobody could stop the Dolphins. Miami beat Washington 14-7 in the Super Bowl. That capped off a season for the history books.

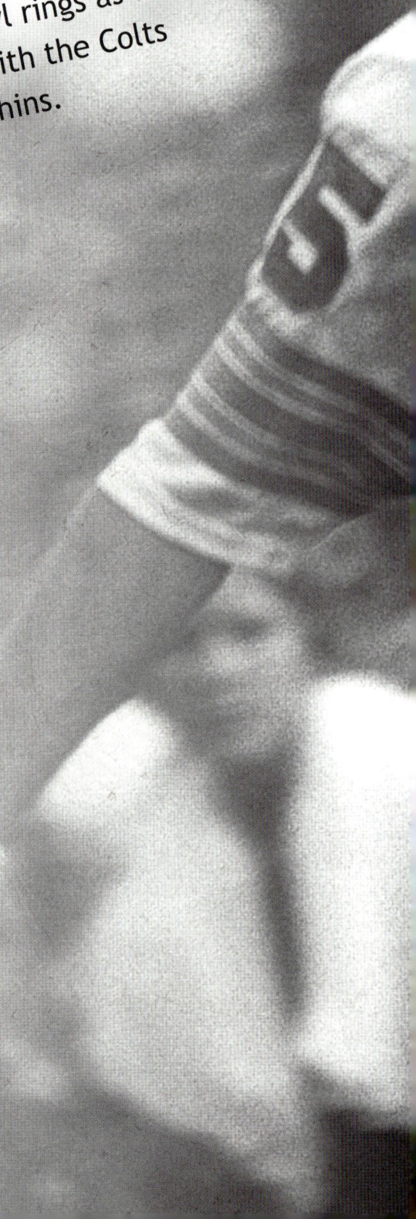

Earl Morrall kept the winning streak going while Bob Griese recovered from a broken leg.

EARLY YEARS

The American Football League (AFL) awarded attorney and businessman Joe Robbie and actor Danny Thomas an expansion team in 1965. But they were not sure where the new team should play. Robbie lived in Minneapolis, Minnesota, but there already was an NFL team there. He thought about putting the team in Philadelphia but ran into the same problem. Then Joe Foss, an old friend of Robbie's and the commissioner of the AFL, told him to check out Miami.

Miami had a stadium—the Orange Bowl—ready to host a pro team.

Two months later, Robbie met with Miami mayor Robert King High. They agreed that the team should begin playing at the Orange Bowl stadium in 1966.

George Wilson was hired as the team's first coach. But they still needed a name. They decided to hold a contest. Fans sent in their favorite ideas. "Dolphins" was the easy winner. The fan who won the contest received two lifetime passes to Dolphins games as her prize.

FAST FACT
In 1957 George Wilson coached the Detroit Lions to the NFL Championship and was the first winner of the NFL Coach of the Year Award.

George Wilson brought a championship track record to Miami.

FAST FACT
Don Shula's Colts reached Super Bowl III, but they were upset by Joe Namath and the New York Jets at Miami's Orange Bowl.

Don Shula arrived in Miami in 1970, and the good times were not far behind him.

HIRING GREATNESS

For their first four seasons, the Dolphins struggled. During that time, they won only 15 games and lost 39, while tying twice. Fans in Florida wanted a winner.

At the end of the 1969 season, Baltimore Colts coach Don Shula was having a disagreement with his team's owner. Joe Robbie convinced Shula to come to Miami. The NFL made the Dolphins give up a first-round draft pick, but Robbie thought Shula was worth it.

He was right. The Dolphins won 10 games in Shula's first season. In 1971, they made it to their first Super Bowl, but they lost to the Dallas Cowboys. By 1972, Miami was the best team in the NFL. Under Shula, the Dolphins were the first team to play in three consecutive Super Bowls.

Shula coached the Dolphins for 26 seasons. He won 328 regular-season games in his career, more than any coach in NFL history.

Don Shula left his mark on the Miami Dolphins like no other person in the team's history.

FAST FACT
Don Shula's sons, David and Mike, both went into coaching just like their dad.

Don Shula led the Dolphins to four Super Bowls and set a record for most NFL victories as a head coach.

Future Hall of Fame guard Larry Little was a big part of the Dolphins' Super Bowl teams in the early 1970s.

BACK-TO-BACK

The Dolphins lost in their first Super Bowl in 1971. But better times were just around the corner.

The next season, Miami became the first team in NFL history to go undefeated and win the Super Bowl. Jim Langer and Larry Little anchored the offensive line. Both would go on to be inducted into the Pro Football Hall of Fame. The "No-Name Defense" had no big stars, just a lot of great players who did their jobs well.

FAST FACT

Besides Larry Little, three other members of the 1972 Dolphins are in the Hall of Fame: fullback Larry Csonka, wide receiver Paul Warfield, and linebacker Nick Buoniconti.

With most of their team back in 1973, the Dolphins lost only two games. They beat the Minnesota Vikings 24-7 in Super Bowl VIII. They were the second team to win back-to-back Super Bowls.

The Dolphins have not won a Super Bowl since then. But their titles in the early 1970s highlighted one of the greatest stretches of play in NFL history.

Larry Csonka, *39*, helped the Dolphins pound the Minnesota Vikings in Super Bowl VIII.

FAST FACT

The only other team to reach three straight Super Bowls is the Buffalo Bills. They went to four in a row, after the 1990–93 seasons.

GETTING A LITTLE LUCKY

The Dolphins went back to the Super Bowl after the 1982 season. They faced Washington again. This time they lost 27-17, but Miami was again one of the best teams in the NFL.

The next spring, the Dolphins had the 27th pick in the NFL Draft. Five quarterbacks were expected to be picked in the first round. One of them was Dan Marino from the University of Pittsburgh.

Fulton Walker returned a kickoff for a touchdown, but the Dolphins lost to Washington in Super Bowl XVII.

Marino had a rocket for an arm, and many thought he would be one of the first players picked. But team after team passed on him. Finally, it was the Dolphins' turn. They already had a decent quarterback, but Marino was too good to pass up. Miami chose Marino, and he became one of the biggest draft steals of all time.

Dan Marino was a fiery competitor who became one of the best quarterbacks the NFL has ever seen.

FAST FACT

Dan Marino was the sixth quarterback taken in the first round of the 1983 NFL Draft.

Baby-faced quarterback Dan Marino took the NFL by storm in 1983.

Dan Marino retired as one of the most productive passers in NFL history.

FAST FACT

Dan Marino was the first NFL quarterback ever to throw for more than 5,000 yards in a season.

Marino played for the Dolphins for 19 years. In just his second season, he set the NFL records for most touchdown passes and passing yards in a season. When he retired in 2000, Marino had more completions, passing yards, and touchdown passes than any player in NFL history. He was inducted into the Pro Football Hall of Fame in 2005.

The Dolphins only made it to one Super Bowl with Marino. They have not been back since the 1984 season. In 2012, they used their first-round draft pick to select a quarterback for the first time since they landed Marino. They took Ryan Tannehill with the eighth overall pick. Tannehill started the first game of his NFL career as the Dolphins looked to make him their next franchise quarterback.

FAST FACT

Bob Griese (12), Dan Marino (13), and Larry Csonka (39) are the only players in Dolphins history to have their numbers retired.

Like Dan Marino, Ryan Tannehill was a first-round draft pick who became the Dolphins' starting quarterback as a rookie.

TIMELINE

1965

The AFL awards an expansion franchise to Joe Robbie and Danny Thomas.

1969

The Dolphins hire Don Shula to coach the team.

1971

The Dolphins advance to their first Super Bowl but lose to the Dallas Cowboys 24-3 on January 16, 1972.

1972

Miami completes the first undefeated season in NFL history, going 14-0 during the regular season and beating Washington 14-7 in Super Bowl VII on January 14, 1973.

1973

The Dolphins defeat the Minnesota Vikings 24-7 in Super Bowl VIII on January 13, 1974.

1983

Quarterback Dan Marino debuts. He goes on to become one of the greatest players in NFL history.

1984

Marino sets NFL records with 5,084 passing yards and 48 touchdown passes. The Dolphins reach the Super Bowl but lose to the San Francisco 49ers.

1996

Shula retires as coach of the Dolphins. His 328 wins are an NFL record.

2000

Marino retires as the NFL's all-time leader in attempts, completions, passing yards, and touchdown passes.

2012

The Dolphins select Ryan Tannehill with their first-round draft pick, and he starts every game at quarterback as a rookie.

GLOSSARY

CONSECUTIVE
Coming in a row, without interruption.

DRAFT
The process by which leagues determine which teams can sign new players coming into the league.

EXPANSION
When a league grows by adding new teams.

FRANCHISE QUARTERBACK
A quarterback who leads a team for a number of years.

INDUCTED
To be admitted as a member to a group.

STEAL
An unexpected bargain.

VETERAN
A player who has played many years.

INDEX

American Football League (AFL), 11

Buoniconti, Nick, 19

Csonka, Larry, 6, 19, 20, 28

Foss, Joe, 11

Griese, Bob, 8, 28

King, Robert, 12

Langer, Jim, 19

Little, Larry, 18, 19

Marino, Dan, 23-24, 25, 26, 27-28

Minneapolis, Minnesota, 11

Morrall, Earl, 8

Morris, Mercury, 6, 7

Namath, Joe, 14

Orange Bowl, 12

Philadelphia, Pennsylvania, 11

Pro Football Hall of Fame, 19, 27

Robbie, Joe, 11-12, 15

Shula, David, 17

Shula, Don, 14, 15-16, 17

Shula, Mike, 17

Super Bowl, 4, 8, 16, 19, 20, 23, 28

Tannehill, Ryan, 28, 29

Thomas, Danny, 11

University of Pittsburgh, 23

Walker, Fulton, 23

Warfield, Paul, 19

Wilson, George, 12

ABOUT THE AUTHOR

Dan Myers was raised in Eagan, Minnesota, and graduated with a degree in journalism from Minnesota State University. He has covered sports at all levels in the Twin Cities since 2008. He and his wife live in Hudson, Wisconsin, with their beagle, Kato.